# The Purple Rain

## The Mockingjay

This is a work of Poetry. Names, characters, businesses, places, events and incidents are either products of the author's imagination or used in a fictitious manner. Any resemblance to actual persons, living or dead, or actual events is purely coincidental.


First Edition: February 2021

Typeset in Adobe Garamond Pro

ISBN: 978-93-90267-60-6

Cover Design: Debabrata Sahoo

Publisher: StoryMirror Infotech Pvt. Ltd.
145, First Floor, Powai Plaza, Hiranandani Gardens, Powai,
Mumbai - 400076, India

Web: https://storymirror.com
Facebook: https://facebook.com/storymirror
Twitter: https://twitter.com/story_mirror
Instagram: https://instagram.com/storymirror
Email: marketing@storymirror.com

# Dedication

Dedicated to My father, Grandma (Dadi), Grandpa (Dada), mother, didi & Abirda, James, Tintin, uncle, aunt, and my unknown Love.

# Preface

"The Purple Rain" - is the title poem of the book and the first poem she wrote of many.

Being a writer means making tough decisions. But she always asked herself that question "why not" for anything that other people said "impossible" or was tagged socially as "should not be done". She always believed and still believes that we all create our own life path; our actions and passion when cross the boundary of ordinary beliefs, conceive creative thinking.

These poems in her book came to her in their entirety. When she questioned each of her life event, she created and got involved in thinking. Her thinking implied creation. She typed out her own thoughts, and feelings. They are all very much honest and real. This is why she is so proud of them.

Maybe this is a bittersweet poetry, but in all, she really wishes you all will be super touched.

## Contents

## The Purple Rain

And silver hailstorm falling from the eave and the trees..
From high bright window,
Looking down I peer like a dreamer over the Rain!
Wander; have you heard my silent scream?
Have you felt my waves?

A paranoid lover,
with an overwhelming desire for unknowns!

*- The Mockingjay*

## Perception

We define it like a shadow in a candlelight,
Only adds to the confusion.
Impossible to see where anyone is!
Outside a storm might be raging,
It feels more of a personal,
It feels as though it has saved all its fury for what is being perceived.

So, perceive nothing.
Perceiving is letting yourself being under control.
Let's not do that, let's just be as free as possible.

*- The Mockingjay*

## Life's Unknown Forces

And strange how you decipher it!
For every word connects to another,
To form an idea, or a purpose.
Or a metaphorical expression.
They've all experienced the unseen forces and connections,
A connection is different;
It's an undeniable voice inside of you,
Like Trust and Love don't have a definite formula,
They happen at a certain Time and Place.
If you believe in Karma at all,
You know – Nothing is a coincidence.

*- The Mockingjay*

## A Shadow Dimension

In those peak hours,
There's a distinctive mood.
And the otherworld comes to life!
In the light and darkness...

Night falls swiftly in the forest on a Rainy evening.
The yellowing glows of fireplace wink,
And surrounding trees reached higher and blacker.
Rain upon the green leaves of trees and
their wet trunks and barks..

You and me, holding hands, our hearts touched,
Sparkling droplets from the sky, and the aroma!
Was it all just a Dream inside a Dream?

*- The Mockingjay*

## The Illumination

And a Glowing blue water washes up on the beach,
Up above, the impenetrably dark sky;
Illuminated with thousand diamonds..
She cleansed her soul, and said..
Wait for me when the Sun blazes hot,
Wait for me when the season changes, and I'm not there.
Wait...even when you can't hear!
Do you trust me?

*- The Mockingjay*

## Blossoms

And when you are here I think of painting out the wall.
time dances in tangent,
slips out like the Butterflies.
Like the blooming flowers in a faded dream!

You came to me gently,
With that unsaid Truth deep in your eyes!

*- The Mockingjay*

## Into the Wilderness

And as the River flows through the land,
The sound of calming water captures our souls,
The immense dark sky is alight with diamond like stars,
Blue, yellow, and pink wildflowers.. grew scattered on the River's side,
A nearby forest, dense and dark..
Green leaves and crimson Red flowers swirl
from the shadow..

And we blaze a campfire,
illuminating the surrounding tranquility,
Warm red-orange flame whipping and
snapping back and forth,
Adjacent rocks were shiny like golden sandpaper,
Silence surrounded and embraced our every being!
Only the River told us its story,
And witnessed the Love we shared!

*- The Mockingjay*

## $4^{th}$ March'20

It's drizzling,
I can hear the rain drops and lightning,
And inside me, such a crucifying pain,
Feels like the blood dripping out.
Brunt the Wall of my Heart…
My eyes are heavy,
Tiredness wrapping me in..
It's going to be a sleepless night.
Waves of the memories drag my consciousness
out of the shadows.

Let it hurt, I'm embracing the burn.
One day it will be numb.

*- The Mockingjay*

## Seashore

Moonless night,
Starry sky,
Silent waves,
Sun-warmed sand,
Bare feet,
Warmth travels through my skin,
Sitting at the beachfront.
A spark of thought...
one thing that always comes in my mind first -
“YOU”

*- The Mockingjay*

## 5th May in Relation to Life's Path 7th June'19

Dad, please come back – was a constant echo at the back of my head.
For past so many days…
For I could realize it just slays.
Living in lie, is far tougher.
Let me embrace this harshness…

Let it slash my heart; let me go into the vortex.
Let me spend all these sleepless nights.
Eventually, we are the greatest definer of our lives.
Dad and Dadi, you will always be in my heart,
Forever; Alive

*- The Mockingjay*

## 17$^{th}$ May in Relation to Life's Path

Darkness,
I've been sinking into its depth,
Ominous, never ending.
You might think I'm sadistic.

For I don't know when I will see the sunshine,
The Evil won, and punished me to Death.
Life & Death; some say it's the universal cosmic law.
I have to accept.
I know I wouldn't be able to write pretty poems these days.
So let me stop here, like a dead-end.
Light & Darkness is my name,
I will come back for you when the eternity's light
will shower me rain!

Dad I miss you so much….

*- The Mockingjay*

## My Only Reason to Smile

Here, I'm fighting a battle like a brave soldier,
Not to give up, even though I feel like I am lost,
On the flip side, life gave me a reason to be grateful for...
Blessed me with the kaleidoscope of blooming flowers!
For I waited half of my life to cherish this beauty!

I wonder they say, God will never take something away,
Unless he did not have something else for you to replace.
Let's live, let these Stars spark!
For we've got only a lifetime to color;

*- The Mockingjay*

## Moonlight and Shadows

Rain soaked street,
Shining silvery grey in the full Moon night!
Down the empty road, Hidden forest,
Woods merging into each other, vaguely out of sight..

My love awakens, Yearning for you..
Like a werewolf; despite the howling storms.

Through the forest, darkness is glowing!
Like it was speaking to a lone wanderer,
Chilly northwest wind rustling through the
mysterious leaves...
Announcing a November Rain.

Catching a surge of passion I look for You my Love,
Through the charcoal black tree leaves,
Through the vast sky, Stars, Moon, and beyond..
In a cold winter full Moon night!

*- The Mockingjay*

## The Brightest Dark

Here I am,
Like a two sided coin,
Have been built through those darkest days.
The other side, I never want you see.
I'll call it as my Past.

It continuously tries to rip my body and soul,
A lump in my throat, wells up those lonely eyes.

When you wrap me in your arms,
The darkness screams within, scared…
Tries to threaten me, reminding me of my Past.

It's a constant battle I live with,
Day and night.
But I chose to only show you my brighter side.

- *The Mockingjay*

## For the Love of My Life,

I want us to be like a Lightning storm,
Dangerous, but beautiful!
An Art in the Sky,
But an Art out of reach!

And for all the struggles and bad times we're going through;
I remember, things will change.
We don't feel this way forever,
Sometimes the hardest lessons are the ones your soul needs
the most in order to make you the best version of Yourself.
Let's be brave and strong as always!

*- The Mockingjay*

## Mistaken Assumptions

From the passion hidden in the lines of her poetry,
To the chaos inside her mind,
You may think it was just the attention that
she was looking for.
But it was only one thing;
she lived for A heart that would understand
the depth of her emotions,
and the moments that would touch her soul.

*- The Mockingjay*

## Take a Moment to Notice

Just be quiet and notice,
Notice the people around you,
And you will find those who would oppress you into doing what they want,
And when you observe, you would find the ones that wants nothing, but just let you be yourself.

*- The Mockingjay*

## A Raging Sea

The emotion I hold for you in the deepest,
Is like a raging Sea,
Powerful and so very deep.
It'll always be.
Through these cyclones, stormy nights and
the heavy rains…
It'll withstand every pain.

*- The Mockingjay*

## When You Love Me,

When you let me know how you Love me,
The waves in my heart make it clear
Just how much you mean to me.
While I'm standing here.. in my balcony,
I listen to my heartbeat, in rhythm with your own.
With every pound that warming sound keeps me safe,
With the Love that you have shown!

*- The Mockingjay*

## A Dreamer!

Standing on the rooftop,
As I watch the flying train passing by,
In the blue sky, high above my head…
Hovering over the streets and the houses,
And into the roof.
I stand speechless, as with a great surprise I knew!

*- The Mockingjay*

## Love Yourself First

And darling, if you have ever loved me, promise me that you will love yourself first.

The heartfelt breeze, after the summer sun goes to sleep,
A feeling that you forgotten for so many years!
Tangled up in those meaningless insecurities,
The power that you hold through your own mind,
You're worthy of a thousand stars!
You're unique!
That everyone does not know how to Love!

*- The Mockingjay*

## My Happy Place

Streaming hot coffee (and a bit more milk)
Clay cups,
You with Me, high on Love!
Old sweaters, timeworn sneakers..
Fragrant candles, old copper coins,
Croaking frogs in rainy evenings,
Heavy rainfall, the smell of rain..
Splashing ponds,
Evergreen trees, chirping grasshoppers in the dense wood,
Scattered books on my bed.

Welcome to my happy place!

*- The Mockingjay*

## Bridges

Yes, You,
You bought me here.
It's time for a confession.
Let me make it clear.

Let me break this Bridge..
Because my Poetry said it all.
You see me?
Do you see the Sinner or a saint?
Somethings aren't meant to be forever.
we don't have to find an answer.
Until you set your old-self free.

*- The Mockingjay*

## A Harsh Downpour

The harsh downpour of the Rain on the roof
and the windows,
And the whistling, roaring wind outside were interrupted by
a blinding streak of lightning,
Followed by a deafening crack of thunder!

This storm had kept her up most of the night,
Yet another streak of lightning, separated by only
milliseconds from its thunder,
interrupted the pound of Rain.
It's dangerous enough to be outside,
the bolts are too near for safety…
but that's how she liked it.
"Safety" is a matter for the mortals.

*- The Mockingjay*

## A New Dawn

A New Dawn is coming,
I feel it in my bones.
Stop playing with your words, I saw the disguise!
I was standing there, watching the hurling flame..
Engulfed my bedroom!
Was it my passion? Or is the form of a destruction, anger,
Change, and rebirth?
All that mattered was a feeling, so adventurous!
Is it that I'm drifting to a place, all treacherous?

*- The Mockingjay*

## The Turning

Ocean,
The way it always attracts the water into Seas,
Throughout all these mess, I firmly believe,
Even if not in this life…
You will end up finding me again in the next.

*- The Mockingjay*

## The Creation

Lightning flashes near me,
Stretching out a raw, uncontrolled power and
energy through my mind, body and soul.
I walk along the coastline..
Searching, for the seashells in this Storm.

On the inside, a message in my subconscious,
For the destruction, and creation of anew!

*- The Mockingjay*

## Re-living – Beyond the Pleasure Principles

Is it a Mind's quest?
Or the sequence of Life repeats itself?
Maybe a simple coincidence!
Let me choose how to describe the next…

You came back to greet me,
And conflict me with my sense of perception!
That circumstance, with an apparent casual connection!
How do I possibly explain..

You are The Love and the pleasure, I always craved for,
The Love that I classified as insurmountable!
But how do I perceive this Reality?
The answer to this question is difficult;
Because, it's the Reality; which would uncover the secrets!

The dimensional state of Existence

Entwined with a quantum world,
Let your thoughts be the guide.
Let it project your Future, your Reality..

*- The Mockingjay*

## Rain Lover

It was about dusk,
I sat idly,
In front of my window.

In the horizon,
Grew up ashy grey rolling clouds.
I smell you, my love.
You are that incoming rain!

Did you hear the thunder rambling now?
So comforting! Let me breath.
Would you come to me?
I can stay up, for hours!
Please let the clouds hang low.
Please let me see you make an Art.
Through the sky, and the trees, and the houses,
and straight into my heart.

*- The Mockingjay*

## The Keys

I'm prisoned in the fortress, high above the mountains,
A tiny thumb of rock fell off into the sea; as the windswept,
Gazing toward the Stars, I wonder..
My mind, faster than the speed of light.

Looking up at the sky, I found comfort…
Let me take solace in the Eternity of the Stars..
The myriad replicas of human mind.

This is for those who are unjustly jailed down on Earth,
Our thoughts are the key,
Brimming with all ideas of created Future Path!

*- The Mockingjay*

## Here's a Message for You

Was it an expression?
There's nothing compared to yours!
You are the one constant in the equation of life!
Let me intersect the secrets of this path.

All of those colors, those lines, those shapes,
In every size;
All of your distortions,
Different; but all enough.

*- The Mockingjay*

## Behind the Camera

What do we look at?
The perspective? Or the memories to capture for Future…
Real Shades,
Things appear to me like there is a revenant.

I can make it as lively as a sketch,
Would I be able to transfer the same feeling just on a click?
Let me avoid any bad clicks, and
with a definite angle making an infinite spirit.

With every sense and vibes from my mind,
Showered from blessed Rain..
To a Rainbow in Your heart.

*- The Mockingjay*

## De'ja' Vu

Designs…for my future?
I've felt my mind is caved in under a maze,
Like a Rose looks like a Rose to everyone,
But when I gaze through; A walk I feel,
A walk through unknowns, begins to form itself.

And that's why I want to explore,
What all these unknown holds?
Now, if you trust me, a very strange runs through me!
So Mysterious! You would hardly believe!

I have lived this moment before,
A thousand of years from now to traverse.
Somethings that feels unfinished,
wants to be known revealing itself!

- *The Mockingjay*

## Clouds

Clouds come floating into my life,
Sometimes to carry rain, or to usher storms.
And other times to add color
In my sunset sky.

*- The Mockingjay*

## The Storm

When the hard wind blows,
When the branches may sway and bend,
But my roots grow deep into the ground,
Connected to the energy of Earth.
My branches are way up high, in the sky..
Reaching to the heavens, strong..

I dream of Autumn, with leaves changing colors..
I'm ready to let go.
Because I know, I will be healthier
in the Spring and in the Summer months.

*- The Mockingjay*

## Distant

You lead me to a very distant land,
Where my Dreams are all faded!
And the air is all stale and gray.

Mysteries and Dreams are all turned to blue, icy cold!
A land where I am not whole,

The vision of a mighty castle across the ocean calls..
It's a secret place, I'm too afraid to touch.

Take me by the hand,
Take me by the Heart,
A place that knows no pain,
Loyalty and Peace, forever ours it will remain.

*- The Mockingjay*

## Moonlight in Thunder

She never thought of this phenomena,
When the Trees are silver shiny and alive,
weirdly illuminated by the Moonlight in Thunder and Snow!
As iced pines exploded and screamed on the breeze.

Metaphysics creating distant cloud illuminating,
of an abrupt thunder.
Her good days Sunshine is always- I, Me, Mine;
and she felt fine.
She's witnessing the precise moment
Of Moonlight by thunderstorm, snow fell like stars filling
the dark trees
Where she swears her Love to freedom and Stars,
Under the vault of dark wide yonder!

*- The Mockingjay*

## Gateway to Heaven

A tender thrill,
I'm safe inside a world of dream!
Wish I could stay here forever!
No going back to the horizon of time.

Separating two paths,
There's so much mystery beyond this field!
Faultless lines of an unknown world,
Composed, ignited and makes me overwhelmed!
a path into another life,
Welcomes you to a shadow realm!

*- The Mockingjay*

## Autumn

Autumn moves so fast through the tunnel of Love.
Surrendered the vines of fences.
A smile around the corner, as bright as the Sun!
...Lures my Mind!

Replaying it in an infinite loop,
My pen writes till I exist.
Dreams are colored by passion!
And radiated by the inner light!

- *The Mockingjay*

## Love Talk

I feel like a bright blue light surrounds me these days.
I'm graceful, strong, and brave.
Enough for not needing a Lover
For the pride or a fate.

Peering through the mirror..
I see a great warrior.
Inspite of all the cuts and the bruises,
Still emanating a raw power;
So overwhelming!
So intoxicating!
Alarmingly strong,
I'm the maddening thunder,
Rippling a darkest storm.

If the society is dangerous and intentful,
Fabricating lies to gain control..
I'll be the lightning storm,
Breaking all darkness and fright,
That resides deep under.

So, let me explore every angle I want to..
Let me grow through mountains,
through the concrete, and rainforests...

In every different directions that gravitate me in,
and I enchant to..
For as I know,
I'm flawed, I'm imperfect..
but inside me there's a wildflower,
Sets a spark, no other can be compared to.

*- The Mockingjay*

## Volcanos

Inside of Me a passion burns so deep,
With thoughts of You..
That flows through my body,
Starts a fire, beyond endurance!

How much is it okay to ask?
How much would it cost to put an end to this fire?

Let the coals cool,
Turn them into ice.
And with it, time could be frozen,
Let me realize,
What would it be like a lifetime!

*- The Mockingjay*

## Let's Run-away

Take my hand,
We will run away, far from here..
Only to come back home, after a while.

- The Mockingjay

## Rain's Kiss

Hidden within the earthly depth,
Only emerges with time.
Only dances in tangent,
Now, slips out with the butterflies.

Rain, would you blow me a kiss out of the dark clouds?
The ones that hid blurring the image on the mirror…

*- The Mockingjay*

## The Chaos

And as I lie down,
In the midst of all chaos..
Just listen to my heart beat...
It echoes only Your name!

*- The Mockingjay*

## A Bright Light

And finally; that bright light inside of
you makes me feel close to myself.
Inhaling, maybe I'm so close to you,
So close to your scent!
Elusive, just lying on my bed,
staring at those gleaming lights.
Let's be together this way !

*- The Mockingjay*

## Unmasking the Mask

Words keep changing, rearranging.
Partiality turns to kindness, when confronted.
Life is short, and all things should reveal.
For the Truth shines without Sun.

Would it crush those wild Dreams?
By such mean extremes?
Maybe..
You never know.

For now; the storm will stray, and everything else stays away.

*- The Mockingjay*

# Thundercloud

Revealing,
The warmth of an August afternoon,
Suddenly broke into a coolest wind..
I held my hands out from the balcony,
And sketch a dreamscape.

I'll sail upon this thundercloud,
Taste the raindrops, touch the stars…
You'll trust my silence then,
when I'll never come back.

The visions I catch in my mind,'
Are the moments from the mountains…
Where we would set ourselves free,
Underneath a hidden beauty,
from a Paradise long forgotten!

*- The Mockingjay*

## The Reunion or a Separation?

On silver screens
Human portray pain.
Cries and tears,
Like that of thunderstorm and rain!

Let me tell you what exactly the pain is,
It's a bittersweet mystery.
A mystery- never clear.
And my heart turns to a flame.
Flickering, riddled glimmer.. beating nevermore!

And I know 'only hate'.

*- The Mockingjay*

## The Transformation

And the autumn is at its peak,
And as it ends when the Sun is swiftly losing its strength in the northern hemisphere,
the nights are becoming longer,
the decay is rapidly occurring as leaves fall from trees,
Plants wither and die, birds migrate to south,
Temperature drops dramatically,
And the silence and the coldness approaches,

I will come into your Life destined for that transformation,
Just like emerging from a crack in the starry sky,
that was buried deep in the darkest part of the Milky Way!

- *The Mockingjay*

**“A life story to be continued..”**

www.ingramcontent.com/pod-product-compliance
Ingram Content Group UK Ltd.
Pitfield, Milton Keynes, MK11 3LW, UK
UKHW040028200726
13854UKWH00001B/421

9 789390 267606